First German
—AT HOME—

Kathy Gemmell and Jenny Tyler
Illustrated by Sue Stitt
Designed by Diane Thistlethwaite

Consultant: Sandy Walker

CONTENTS

3 Speaking German

4 The Strudels

6 At home

8 Draw a map

10 Counting in German

12 Jigsaw puzzles

14 What is it?

16 A day in the life
   of the Strudels

18 Afternoon activity

20 Happy birthday

22 Silvia goes shopping

24 Market day

26 Dominoes to make

28 Memory game

30 Word list

32 Answers

First published in 1993 by Usborne Publishing Ltd.
Usborne House, 83-85 Saffron Hill
London EC1N 8RT, England.
Copyright © 1993 Usborne Publishing Ltd.
First published in America August 1993.
Printed in Portugal.
Universal Edition.

Speaking German

This book is about the Strudel family. They are going to help you learn to speak German.

Word lists

You will find a word list on every double page to tell you what the German words mean.

Guten Tag
gootn tahg

The little letters are to help you say the German words. Read them as if they were English words.

Hallo
hullaw

Word list

Guten Tag gootn tahg	hello
Hallo hullaw	hi
nein nine	no
ja yah	yes
ich ikh	I
Tschüß tshewss	bye!
du bist dran doo bist dran	your turn

The best way to find out how to say German words is to listen to a German person speaking. Some letters and sounds are a bit different from English. Here are some clues to help you.

When you see a "ch" in German, it is written "kh" in the little letters. Say this like the "h" in "huge". Try saying *ich*, which means "I".

Say "sch" like the "sh" sound in "show".

When you see one of these: ß, just say it like a double "s".

To say the ü, round your lips to say "oo" then say "ee" instead.

The letter "j" in German sounds like the English "y".

Try saying out loud what each person on this page is saying.

See if you can find Josefina the mouse on each double page.

Ich...
ikh

Tschüß
tshewss

Nein
nine

Ja
yah

Games with word lists

You can play games with the word lists if you like. Here are some ideas.

1. Cover all the German words and see if you can say the German for each English word. Score a point for each one you can remember.

2. Time yourself and see if you can say the whole list more quickly next time.

3. Race a friend. The first one to say the German for each word scores a point. The winner is the one to score the most points.

4. Play all these games the other way around, saying the English for each German word.

Du bist dran
Look for the *du bist dran* boxes in this book. There is something for you to do in each of them. *Du bist dran* means "your turn".

Look out for the joke bubbles on some of the pages.

The Strudels

Here the Strudel family are introducing themselves. *Ich heiße* [ikh hyssa] means "I am called" or "my name is".

Bella has chased Josefina through the Strudel's garden. See if you can follow her route from Onkel Helmut to where she is now. Which members of the family did she pass on the way?

Word list

ich heiße ikh hyssa	I am called
Herr hair	Mr.
Frau fraow	Mrs.
Oma awma	Granny
Onkel onkel	uncle
Tante tanta	aunt
Guten Morgen gootn more gn	good morning
Auf Wiedersehen owf veederzane	goodbye

Names

Strudel shtroodel	**Helmut** helmoot
Rainer ryner	**Max** mux
Silvia zilveeya	**Bella** bella
Markus mahrkoos	**Josefina** yawzefeena
Uli oolee	**Franz** frunts
Karin kahrin	**Hans** hunts
Ilse ilza	**Katja** katya

Ich heiße Silvia.

Ich heiße Rainer.

Ich heiße Max.

Ich heiße Uli.

Ich heiße Oma Strudel.

Ich heiße Katja.

Ich heiße Markus.

Good morning

Guten Morgen [gootn more gn] means "good morning". Silvia is so sleepy, she has mixed up everyone's names. Say *Guten Morgen* for her, adding the correct name each time.

Guten Morgen Markus

Guten Morgen Oma

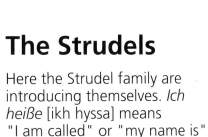

4

5

At home

Here is the inside of the Strudel family house. Can you find a way around the house, passing all those who are waiting to tell you the names of the rooms on the way? You must not pass anyone more than once.

Start at the door nearest Frau Strudel and go out by the kitchen door. (Remember that doors are not the only way to get from room to room.)

Bei uns [by oonts] means "at our home". "At my home" is *bei mir* [by meer]. At anyone else's home is *bei* then the name of the person, so "at Silvia's home" would be *bei Silvia* [by zilveeya].

Word list

hier ist	here is
here ist	
das Schlafzimmer	bedroom
dass shlahf tsimmer	
das Badezimmer	bathroom
dass bahda tsimmer	
die Mansarde	attic
dee man sarda	
der Keller	cellar
dare keller	
die Küche	kitchen
dee kewkha	
das Wohnzimmer	lounge
dass vawn tsimmer	
das Eßzimmer	dining room
dass ess tsimmer	
das Haus	house
dass howss	
der Garten	garden
dare gartn	
Mutti	mum
moottee	
bei uns	at our home
by oonts	

Hier ist das Schlafzimmer.

Hier ist das Wohnzimmer.

Hier ist der Garten.

Hier ist Mutti.

Hier ist das Haus.

Draw a map

Silvia and Markus have drawn a map of the area near their house and have written all the names in German.

Draw a map of your own area or somewhere you think you would like to live and label it in German.

die Kirche

die Brücke

der Fluß

der Bauernhof

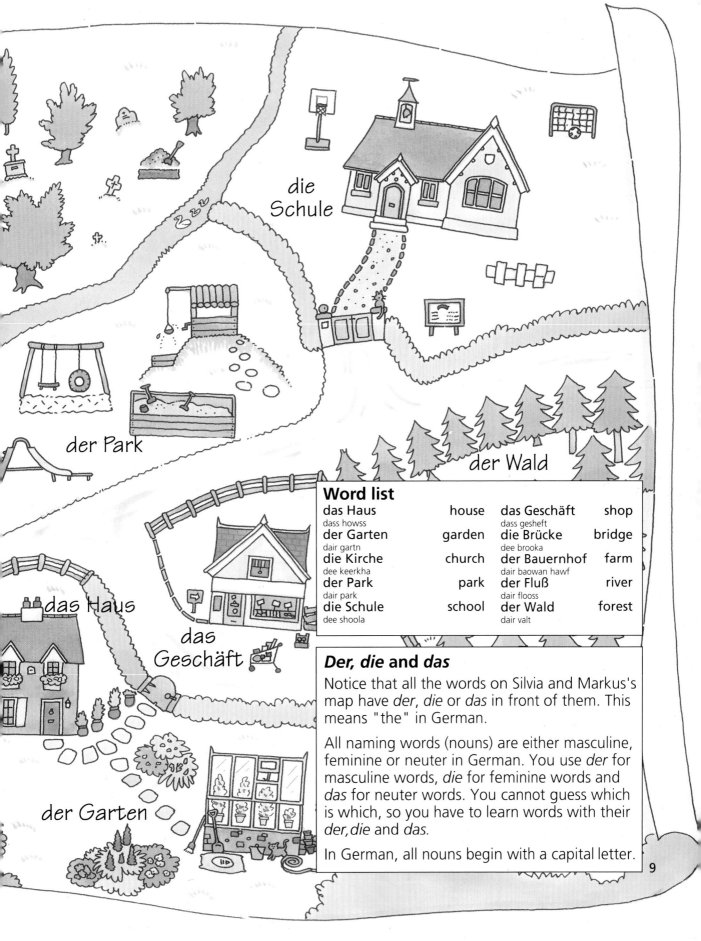

die Schule

der Park

der Wald

das Haus

das Geschäft

der Garten

Word list

das Haus dass howss	house	**das Geschäft** dass gesheft	shop
der Garten dair gartn	garden	**die Brücke** dee brooka	bridge
die Kirche dee keerkha	church	**der Bauernhof** dair baowan hawf	farm
der Park dair park	park	**der Fluß** dair flooss	river
die Schule dee shoola	school	**der Wald** dair valt	forest

Der, die and *das*

Notice that all the words on Silvia and Markus's map have *der*, *die* or *das* in front of them. This means "the" in German.

All naming words (nouns) are either masculine, feminine or neuter in German. You use *der* for masculine words, *die* for feminine words and *das* for neuter words. You cannot guess which is which, so you have to learn words with their *der, die* and *das.*

In German, all nouns begin with a capital letter.

Counting in German

Silvia and Markus stayed up late to finish their map and now can't sleep. In fact, everybody is counting things to help them get to sleep.

Count out loud in German for each person. Who do you think fell asleep first? Use the number list to help you.

Number list

eins ine ts	one
zwei tsvy	two
drei dry	three
vier feer	four
fünf foonf	five
sechs zex	six
sieben zee bn	seven
acht akht	eight
neun noyn	nine
zehn tsain	ten

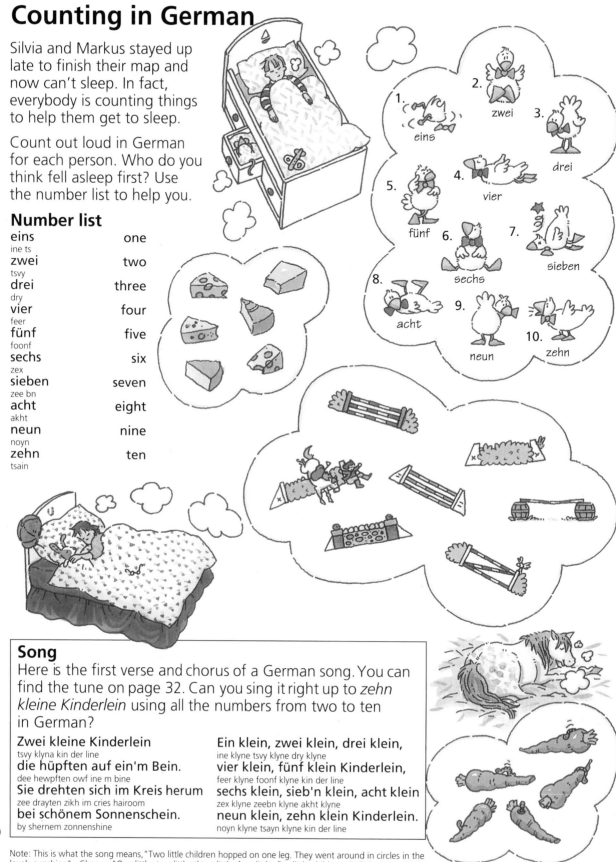

Song

Here is the first verse and chorus of a German song. You can find the tune on page 32. Can you sing it right up to *zehn kleine Kinderlein* using all the numbers from two to ten in German?

Zwei kleine Kinderlein
tsvy klyna kin der line
die hüpften auf ein'm Bein.
dee hewpften owf ine m bine
Sie drehten sich im Kreis herum
zee drayten zikh im cries hairoom
bei schönem Sonnenschein.
by shernem zonnenshine

Ein klein, zwei klein, drei klein,
ine klyne tsvy klyne dry klyne
vier klein, fünf klein Kinderlein,
feer klyne foonf klyne kin der line
sechs klein, sieb'n klein, acht klein
zex klyne zeebn klyne akht klyne
neun klein, zehn klein Kinderlein.
noyn klyne tsayn klyne kin der line

10

Note: This is what the song means, "Two little children hopped on one leg. They went around in circles in the lovely sunshine". Chorus: "One little, two little, three little, four little, five little children, six little, seven little, eight little, nine little, ten little children."

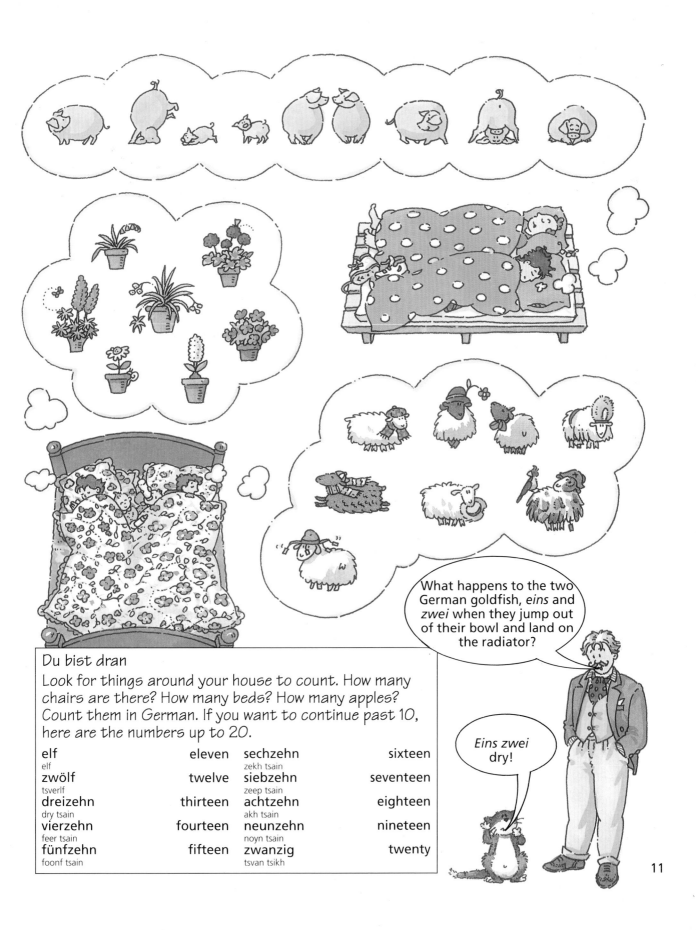

Du bist dran

Look for things around your house to count. How many chairs are there? How many beds? How many apples? Count them in German. If you want to continue past 10, here are the numbers up to 20.

elf		eleven	**sechzehn**		sixteen
elf			zekh tsain		
zwölf		twelve	**siebzehn**		seventeen
tsverlf			zeep tsain		
dreizehn		thirteen	**achtzehn**		eighteen
dry tsain			akh tsain		
vierzehn		fourteen	**neunzehn**		nineteen
feer tsain			noyn tsain		
fünfzehn		fifteen	**zwanzig**		twenty
foonf tsain			tsvan tsikh		

What happens to the two German goldfish, *eins* and *zwei* when they jump out of their bowl and land on the radiator?

Eins zwei dry!

11

Jigsaw puzzles

The next morning everybody is tired and a little bit grumpy. Rainer has brought down some jigsaw puzzles to try and cheer up the family. However, the pieces are all mixed up and Markus is the only one who can see what his puzzle is, *ein Apfel* (an apple).

Can you say in German what all the other puzzles should be? Use the picture list to help you. Only one of the missing pieces cannot be found anywhere. Who will not be able to finish their jigsaw?

Ein, eine and *eins*

In German there are two ways to say "a" something or "one" something, *ein* or *eine*. All *der* and *das* words are *ein* words and all *die* words are *eine* words. To say "one" when you are counting, you say *eins* [ine ts].

Ein
Apfel

Picture list

eine Pflaume
ine a pflaow ma
a plum

eine Ananas
ine a ananass
a pineapple

eine Banane
ine a banana
a banana

ein Pfirsich
ine pfeer zikh
a peach

eine Birne
ine a beerna
a pear

eine Apfelsine
ine a apfull zeena
an orange

ein Apfel
ine ap full
an apple

Du bist dran
See if you can remember the words for all these fruits and say what's in your fruit bowl at home.

12

Answer these questions out loud in German.

Can you see what Josefina is eating? What would Max like to eat?

Song

Here is a song about the fruit and vegetables that Josefina likes and dislikes. Can you guess what any of them are? You can see what all the words mean on page 32.

Kopf - sa - lat und Gur - ke frißt Jo - se - fi - na gern,
kopf za laht oont goor ka frist yaw za fee na gairn

A - ber Blu - men - kohl und Boh - nen nicht so sehr.
ah ber bloo men kawl oont baw nen nikht zaw zair

Sie mag Pam - pel - mu - se, An - an - as und Birn',
zee mahg pum pull moo za an an ass oont beern

A - ber ih - re Erb - sen gibt sie al - le mir.
ah ber ee ra airb sen geept zee al la meer

13

Joke: What's blue and square? An orange in disguise.

What is it?

Oma has ordered lots of new things for her room. They have just been delivered. *Was ist das?* [vass ist dass] means "what is it?" or "what is that?".

Can you help the rest of the family say in German what is in each parcel? Say *das ist* [dass ist] which means "it is" and then the object. Use the picture list to help you with the names.

Remember that *ein* and *eine* both mean "one" or "a".

Picture list

ein Tisch
ine tish
a table

ein Stuhl
ine shtool
a chair

ein Bett
ine bet
a bed

ein Fernseher
ine fairn zayer
a television

eine Vase
ine a vahza
a vase

ein Wecker
ine vecker
an alarm clock

eine Lampe
ine a lampa
a lamp

eine Tasse
ine a tassa
a cup

ein Teller
ine teller
a plate

Du bist dran
Can you find all the things on the picture list in your own house? If you can, point to each one and say what it is in German, using *das ist* [dass ist] and then the name of the object.

Joke: What's this? It's this the other way around.

A day in the life of the Strudels

This is a picture strip of a typical weekend day in the Strudel household - after a good night's sleep this time - but the pictures are all in the wrong order. Can you decide which order they should be in?

Use the word list to help you to say out loud what everyone is saying.

Word list

das Frühstück *dass frew shtook*	breakfast
das Mittagessen *dass mittah gessn*	lunch
das Abendessen *dass ah bnd essn*	dinner
morgens *more gns*	in the morning
nachmittags *nakh mittahks*	in the afternoon
Guten Morgen *gootn more gn*	good morning
Guten Abend *gootn ah bnd*	good evening
Gute Nacht *goota nakht*	good night
schlaf gut *shlahf goot*	sleep well
es ist 3 Uhr *ess ist dry oor*	it is three o'clock
es ist 8 Uhr *ess ist akht oor*	it is eight o'clock

Here is a little rhyme about Franz. Can you spot him in two of the pictures?

> **Das kleine Kaninchen**
> *dass klyna ka neen khn*
> **Steht auf um sieben**
> *shtate owf oom zeebn*
> **Abends um acht**
> *ah bnds oom akht*
> **Sagt "gute Nacht ".**
> *zahkt goota nakht*

You can check what all the
16 words mean on page 32.

Guten Appetit [gootn appa teet] is what you say before eating in Germany. It means "enjoy your meal".

Essen kommen [essn kommn] is how you tell people in German to come and eat.

17

Afternoon activity

This afternoon the Strudels are all busy doing things in and around the house. Can you find someone doing each of the things on the word list somewhere in the big picture?

As you find each one, read out loud what that person is saying in German.

Word list

ich esse *ikh essa*	I am eating
ich lese *ikh layza*	I am reading
ich laufe *ikh laowfa*	I am running
ich gehe *ikh gaya*	I am walking
ich singe *ikh zinga*	I am singing
ich trinke *ikh trinka*	I am drinking
ich spreche *ikh shprekha*	I am speaking
ich schlafe *ikh shlahfa*	I am sleeping
ich arbeite *ikh ahr byta*	I am working
ich schwimme *ikh shvimma*	I am swimming
ich falle *ikh falla*	I am falling
ich gehe aus *ikh gaya owss*	I am going out
ich springe *ikh shpringa*	I am jumping

Du bist dran

Was machst du? [vass makhst doo]. What are you doing at the moment? You're probably reading, so you say *ich lese* [ich layza]. See if you can do all the other things in the picture and remember how to say them in German.

18

Joke: What has eight legs and spins? A spider in a washing machine.

Happy birthday

The next day is Oma's birthday and the family is having a party for her. There are lots of different kinds of food because everyone likes different things.

To say you like something in German you say *ich mag* [ikh mahg] and then the thing you like. To say you don't like something you say the thing you don't like and then *mag ich nicht* [mahg ikh nikht].

"Happy birthday" in German is *Herzlichen Glückwunsch zum Geburtstag* [hairtslikhn glookvoontsh tsoom gaboorts tahg].

Ich mag Schinken.

Herzlichen Glückwunsch zum Geburtstag.

Ich mag Brot.

Ich mag Marmelade.

Ich mag Pralinen.

Word list

ich mag *ikh mahg*	I like
...mag ich nicht *mahg ikh nikht*	I don't like...
Obst *awpst*	fruit
Käse *kayza*	cheese
Brot *brawt*	bread
Gemüse *gamooza*	vegetables
Marmelade *marmalahda*	jam
Pralinen *prah leenan*	chocolates
Salat *zallaht*	salad
Schinken *shinkan*	ham
Suppe *zooppa*	soup
Pommes frites *pom frit*	french fries
Torten *tortn*	cakes
Würstchen *verst khen*	sausages

Can you see which people do not like the food in front of them? Say out loud in German what they are thinking.

What do you think Silvia is saying? How would Max say what he likes in German?

In German most cakes are called *Torten* but some sponge cakes are called *Kuchen* [kookhen].

Silvia goes shopping

Today is a school holiday and Silvia has gone to do the shopping.

Can you see from the picture what Silvia is asking for? *Ich möchte* [ikh merkhte] means "I would like" and *und* [oont] means "and".

Now try to ask for all the items on Silvia's shopping list in German. Remember to say "please", *bitte* [bitta] and "thank you", *danke schön* [dunka shern].

Der, *die* and *das* all change to *die* when you are talking about more than one thing. The name of the thing usually changes a bit as well.

> Ich möchte eine Zeitung und ein Eis, bitte.

Liste
4 Äpfel
9 Bananen
8 Brötchen
5 Zwiebeln
6 Fische
2 Torten

Can you see from the picture how to say "How much does that come to?" in German? Say it out loud.

What do you think Uli will ask for? Say it for him.

Number reminder

eins	one	sechs	six
ine ts		zex	
zwei	two	sieben	seven
tsvy		zee bn	
drei	three	acht	eight
dry		akht	
vier	four	neun	nine
feer		noyn	
fünf	five	zehn	ten
foonf		tsain	

Du bist dran

Wieviel [vee feel] means "how much" in German and *wieviele* [vee feela] means "how many". Can you answer the following questions by looking at the picture? Use the number reminder to help you count up in German how many there are.

Wieviele Blumen? (flowers)
Wieviele Hüte? (hats)
Wieviele Katzen? (cats)

22

Note: The money used in Germany is German Marks, called *Deutschmark* (DM), and *Pfennigs* (Pf). There are 100 Pfennigs to a Mark.

Word list

ich möchte (ikh merkhte)	I would like
die Katze (dee katsa)	cat
der Apfel (dair apfull)	apple
die Banane (dee banana)	banana
das Brötchen (dass brert khen)	roll
die Zwiebel (dee tsveebel)	onion
das macht...Mark (dass makht...mark)	that's...Mark
wieviel macht das? (vee feel makht dass)	how much does that come to?
der Fisch (dair fish)	fish
die Blume (dee blooma)	flower
die Torte (dee torta)	cake
das Eis (dass ice)	ice cream cone
bitte (bitta)	please
danke schön (dunka shern)	thank you
der Hut (dair hoot)	hat
die Zeitung (dee tsy toong)	newspaper

Joke: Which dogs don't bite? Hot dogs.

23

Market day

Later on, the whole family goes down to the market. Everybody in the village seems to be there. It is so crowded that the Strudels have split up and are all doing things in different parts of the market.

Uli asks where Franz is and the butcher points to him. *Wo ist* [vaw ist] means "where is" and *da ist Franz* [dah ist frunts] means "there's Franz".

Can you spot all of the Strudels in the crowd? Point to each one and say *da ist* [dah ist] followed by the person's name.

Wo ist Bella?

Wo ist Max?

Wo ist Josefina?

Wo ist Franz?

Da ist Franz.

Danke schön

Wo gehst du hin?
vaw gayst
doo hin

Ich ziehe um.
ikh tseeya oom

24

Joke: Where are you going? I'm moving (house).

Dominoes to make

For something to do at home, Silvia and Markus have invented a game of dominoes which uses German colours. Here's how to make one like theirs and play it.

1. Cut your cardboard into 28 rectangles about 8cm long and 4cm wide (3in by 1½in). You can make the rectangles bigger if you have more cardboard.

4cm
8cm

You will need:
white cardboard (at least 32cm by 28 cm, 13in by 11in), felt tips, scissors and a black pen.

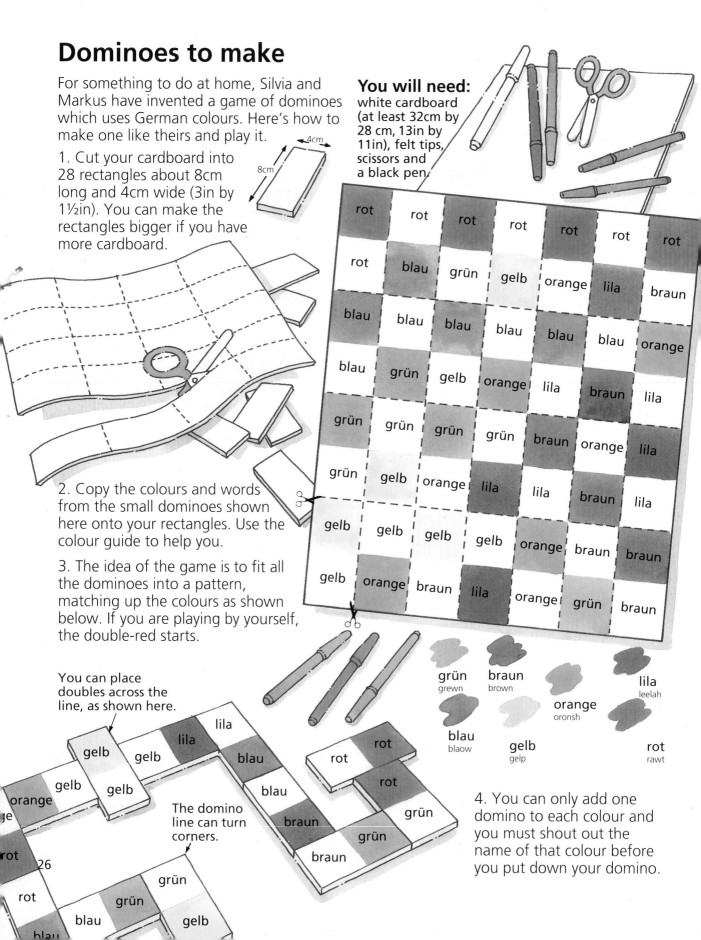

rot	rot	rot	rot	rot	rot	rot
rot	blau	grün	gelb	orange	lila	braun
blau	blau	blau	blau	blau	blau	orange
blau	grün	gelb	orange	lila	braun	lila
grün	grün	grün	grün	braun	orange	lila
grün	gelb	orange	lila	lila	braun	lila
gelb	gelb	gelb	gelb	orange	braun	braun
gelb	orange	braun	lila	orange	grün	braun

2. Copy the colours and words from the small dominoes shown here onto your rectangles. Use the colour guide to help you.

3. The idea of the game is to fit all the dominoes into a pattern, matching up the colours as shown below. If you are playing by yourself, the double-red starts.

You can place doubles across the line, as shown here.

gelb · gelb
gelb · gelb
orange
lila · lila
blau · blau
braun

The domino line can turn corners.

rot · rot
rot · rot
braun
grün
grün
braun

grün grewn **braun** brown **lila** leelah

orange oronsh

blau blaow **gelb** gelp **rot** rawt

4. You can only add one domino to each colour and you must shout out the name of that colour before you put down your domino.

rot
26
rot
grün
blau · gelb
blau

5. If you are playing with a friend, first spread the dominoes out, face-down, on the table or floor. Take seven dominoes each and put them face-up in front of you. These form your "hand".

6. The idea of this game is to get rid of all the dominoes in your hand and the first person to do so is the winner.

Du bist dran.

7. The first person to put down a double and shout out what colour it is (in German) starts. Take turns to match your dominoes with the colours or colour words at either end of the domino line, each time shouting out the colour in German before putting down your domino.

8. If you can't go, you must pick up a spare domino if there is one left, or miss a turn if there is not.

Word list
du bist dran doo bist dran	your turn
ich habe gewonnen ikh hahba gavonnen	I've won

Ich habe gewonnen.

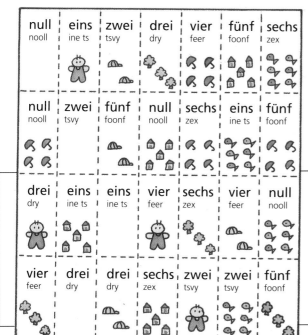

null nooll	eins ine ts	zwei tsvy	drei dry	vier feer	fünf foonf	sechs zex
null nooll	zwei tsvy	fünf foonf	null nooll	sechs zex	eins ine ts	fünf foonf
drei dry	eins ine ts	eins ine ts	vier feer	sechs zex	vier feer	null nooll
vier feer	drei dry	drei dry	sechs zex	zwei tsvy	zwei tsvy	fünf foonf

Number dominoes

You could also make German number dominoes. Copy these dominoes onto pieces of cardboard (the same as the ones used for Colour dominoes) and play in the same way, this time matching up the number of objects with the number in German. The double-six fish starts.

Memory game

Here is a game which you can play again and again. The idea is to get to the finish as quickly as possible.

You will need:

a dice
a clock or watch

How to play

Look at the time when you start. Throw the dice and count with your finger the number of squares shown on the dice. Say the answer to the question on that square out loud then shake again.

If you land on a square with no question on it, shake again and move on.

All the answers can be found in this book, so if you can't remember or are not sure, look through the book until you find the correct answer.

Look at the time again when you finish. Can you do it more quickly next time?

Which way would you say *die Kirche*?

1. dye keerkha
2. dee keerkha
3. dee kersha

Tell Markus how to ask for an ice cream cone in German.

Wieviele Blumen?

Say "yes" in German.

Say "hi" in German.

What would Markus say if you asked, *Was machst du?*

Was ist das?

How do you introduce yourself in German?

1. rot
2. lila
3. gelb

Say "hello" in German.

Which of these describes Katja's balloon?

What is Silvia saying to Herr Grün?

Say "good night" in German.

Which of these is Silvia saying?

Say "I am eating" in German.

1. Ich mag Käse
2. Ich mag Schinken
3. Ich mag Pralinen

How will Markus tell his friend what Josefina's name is?

Start
shtart
(start)

28

Word list

Here is a list of all the German words and phrases used in this book in alphabetical order. You can use the list either to check quickly what a word means, or to test yourself. Cover up any German or English word or phrase and see if you can say its translation. (Remember that some words change slightly when you are talking about more than one thing.)

German	Pronunciation	English
Abendessen (das)	ah bnd essn	*dinner*
abends	ah bnds	*in the evening*
aber	ah ber	*but*
acht	akht	*eight*
achtzehn	akh tsain	*eighteen*
Ananas (die)	ananass	*pineapple*
Apfel (der)	ap full	*apple*
Äpfel (die)	ep full	*apples*
Apfelsine (die)	ap full zeena	*orange*
Auf Wiedersehen	owf veederzane	*goodbye*
Badezimmer (das)	bahda tsimmer	*bathroom*
Banane (die)	banana	*banana*
Bauernhof (der)	baowan hawf	*farm*
bei mir	by meer	*at my home*
Bein (das)	bine	*leg*
Bett (das)	bet	*bed*
Birne (die)	beerna	*pear*
bitte	bitta	*please*
blau	blaow	*blue*
Blume (die)	blooma	*flower*
Blumenkohl (der)	bloo men kawl	*cauliflower*
Bohnen (die)	baw nen	*beans*
braun	brown	*brown*
Brot (das)	brawt	*bread*
Brötchen (das)	brert khen	*roll*
Brücke (die)	brooka*	*bridge*
da ist (Franz)	dah ist (frunts)	*there's (Franz)*
danke schön	dunka shern	*thank you very much*
das ist	dass ist	*it/that is*
das macht...Mark	dass makht..mark	*that makes...Marks*
der, die, das	dair, dee, dass	*the*
drei	dry	*three*
dreizehn	dry tsain	*thirteen*
du bist dran	doo bist dran	*your turn*
ein, eine	ine, ine a	*a/an/one*
eins	ine ts	*one*
Eis (das)	ice	*ice cream cone*
elf	elf	*eleven*
er	air	*he*
er dreht sich	air drayt zikh	*he spins*
er heißt	air hyste	*he is called*

German	Pronunciation	English
er sagt	air zahkt	*he says*
er steht auf	air shtate owf	*he gets up*
Erbsen (die)	airb sen	*peas*
es	ess	*it*
es ist ...Uhr	ess ist...oor	*it is...o'clock*
essen kommen	essn kommn	*come and eat*
E@@@ßzimmer (das)	ess tsimmer	*dining room*
Fernseher (der)	fairn zayer	*television*
Fisch (der)	fish	*fish*
Fluß (der)	flooss*	*river*
Frau	fraow	*Mrs.*
Frühstück (das)	frew shtook*	*breakfast*
fünf	foonf*	*five*
fünfzehn	foonf tsain*	*fifteen*
Garten (der)	gartn	*garden*
gelb	gelp	*yellow*
Gemüse (das)	gamooza	*vegetables*
Geschäft (das)	gesheft	*shop*
grün	grewn	*green*
Gurke (die)	goorka	*cucumber*
Guten Abend	gootn ah bnd	*good evening*
Guten Appetit	gootn appateet	*enjoy your meal*
Guten Morgen	gootn more gn	*good morning*
Gute Nacht	goota nakht	*good night*
Guten Tag	gootn tahg	*hello*
Hallo	hullaw	*hi*
Haus (das)	howss	*house*
Herr	hair	*Mr.*
Herzlichen Glückwunsch zum Geburtstag	hairtslikhn glookvoontsh* tsoom* gaboorts tahg	*happy birthday*
hier ist	here ist	*here is*
Hund (der)	hoont*	*dog*
Hut (der)	hoot	*hat*
ich	ikh	*I*
ich arbeite	ikh ahr byta	*I am working*
ich esse	ikh essa	*I am eating*
ich falle	ikh falla	*I am falling*
ich gehe	ikh gaya	*I am walking*
ich gehe aus	ikh gaya owss	*I am going out*
ich habe gewonnen	ikh hahba gavonnen	*I've won*
ich heiße	ikh hyssa	*I am called*
ich laufe	ikh laowfa	*I am running*
ich lese	ikh layza	*I am reading*
ich mag	ikh mahg	*I like*
ich möchte	ikh merkhta	*I would like*
ich schlafe	ikh shlahfa	*I am sleeping*
ich schwimme	ikh shvimma	*I am swimming*
ich singe	ikh zinga	*I am singing*

30

*The 'oo' sound in these words is like the 'u' in 'put'.

German	Pronunciation	English
ich spreche	ikh shprekha	I am speaking
ich springe	ikh shpringa	I am jumping
ich trinke	ikh trinka	I am drinking
ich ziehe um	ikh tseeya oom*	I am moving (house)
im Kreis	im cries	in a circle
ja	yah	yes
Kaninchen (das)	ka neen khn	rabbit
Käse (der)	kayza	cheese
Katze (die)	katsa	cat
Keller (der)	keller	cellar
Kirche (die)	keerkha	church
kleine	klyna	little
Kopfsalat (der)	kopf za laht	lettuce
Küche (die)	kewkha	kitchen
Lampe (die)	lampa	lamp
lila	leelah	purple
Liste (die)	lissta	list
mag ich nicht	mahg ikh nikht	I don't like
Mansarde (die)	man sarda	attic
Marmelade (die)	marmalahda	jam
Mittagessen (das)	mittah gessn	lunch
morgens	more gns	in the morning
Mutti	moottee*	mum
nachmittags	nakh mittahks	in the afternoon
nein	nine	no
neun	noyn	nine
neunzehn	noyn tsain	nineteen
null	nooll*	zero
Obst (das)	awpst	fruit
Oma (die)	awma	grandma
Onkel (der)	onkel	uncle
orange	oronsh	orange
Pampelmuse (die)	pum pull mooza	grapefruit
Park (der)	park	park
Pfirsich (der)	pfeer zikh	peach
Pflaume (die)	pflaow ma	plum
Pralinen (die)	prah leenan	chocolates
Pommes frites (die)	pom frit	french fries
rot	rawt	red
Salat (der)	zallaht	salad
schlaf gut	shlahf goot	sleep well
Schlafzimmer (das)	shlahf tsimmer	bedroom
Schinken (der)	shinkan	ham
schön	shern	lovely
Schule (die)	shoola	school
sechs	zex	six
sechzehn	zekh tsain	sixteen
sie	zee	she
sieben	zeebn	seven
siebzehn	zeep tsain	seventeen
sie heißt	zee hyste	she is called
Spinne (die)	shpinna	spider
Start	shtart	start
Stuhl (der)	shtool	chair
Suppe (die)	zooppa*	soup
Tante (die)	tanta	aunt
Tasse (die)	tassa	cup
Teller (der)	teller	plate
Tisch (der)	tish	table
Torte (die)	torta	cake
Tschüß	tshewss	bye
um	oom*	at
umgekehrt	oom gekairt*	the other way around
und	oont*	and
Vase (die)	vahza	vase
Vati	fahtee	dad
verkleidete	fairklydet a	in disguise
vier	feer	four
viereckig	feer eckig	square
vierzehn	feer tsain	fourteen
Wald (der)	valt	wood
was ist das?	vass ist dass	what is it/that?
was machst du?	vass makhst doo	what are you doing?
was magst du?	vass mahgst doo	what do you like?
was magst du nicht?	vass mahgst doo nicht	what do you not like?
Waschmaschine (die)	vashma sheena	washing machine
Wecker (der)	vecker	alarm clock
welche..?	vellkha	which..?
wieviele?	vee feela	how many?
wieviel macht das?	vee feel makht dass	how much does that come to?
wo gehst du hin?	vaw gayst doo hin	where are you going?
Wohnzimmer (das)	vawn tsimmer	living room
wo ist..?	vaw ist	where is..?
Würstchen (das)	verst khen	sausage
zehn	tsain	ten
Zeitung (die)	tsy toong*	newspaper
Ziel	tseel	end
zwanzig	tsvan tsikh	twenty
zwei	tsvy	two
Zwiebel (die)	tsveebel	onion
zwölf	tsverlf	twelve

Answers

PAGE 4-5

Bella passed *Onkel Helmut, Herr Strudel, Franz, Tante Ilse, Uli, Rainer, Silvia, Max, Katja, Markus, Oma* and *Frau Strudel.*

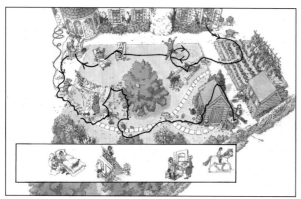

Silvia should say *Guten Morgen Bella, Guten Morgen Markus* and *Guten Morgen Oma.*

PAGE 6-7

This is the way you must go:

PAGE 10-11

Max fell asleep first - he only counted to five before falling asleep. The tune for the song is:

Sechs klein, sieb'n klein, acht klein, neun klein, zehn klein Kin-der - lein.
zex klyne zeebn klyne akht klyne noyn klyne tsayn klyne kin der line

PAGE 12-13

What everyone's jigsaws were:
Herr Strudel-*ein Pfirsich* (a peach),
Tante Ilse-*eine Birne* (a pear),
Karin-*eine Banane* (a banana),
Katja-*eine Ananas* (a pineapple),
Uli-*eine Pflaume* (a plum),
Silvia-*eine Apfelsine* (an orange).

Herr Strudel will not be able to finish his jigsaw.

The answers to the questions are:
Josefina - *eine Pflaume* (a plum),
Max - *ein Apfel* (an apple).

Here is what the words of the song mean in English:
Josefina likes eating
Lettuce and cucumber,
But she doesn't like
Cauliflower and beans much.
She likes grapefruit,
Pineapple and pear,
But all her peas,
She gives to me.

PAGE 16-17

The right order for the pictures is: D F G H B E C A

Here is the rhyme in English:
The little rabbit
Gets up at seven,
In the evening at eight
(He) says "goodnight".

PAGE 20-21

Markus is thinking *Käse mag ich nicht.*
Rainer is thing *Suppe mag ich nicht.*
Onkel Helmut is thinking *Würstchen mag ich nicht.*
Silvia is saying *Ich mag Pommes frites.*
Max would say *Ich mag Obst.*

PAGE 22-23

Silvia is asking for a newspaper and an ice cream cone.

"How much is it?" is *wieviel macht das?*
Uli is going to say *Ich möchte ein Eis, bitte.*

There are:
9 *Blumen*
5 *Hüte*
6 *Katzen*